written by Dawn McMillan
illustrated by Pauline Whimp

1

Luke didn't like reading.
"I'm not good at it," he said
to his teacher, Miss Davidson.

"Don't give up, Luke," said Miss Davidson. "Come with me. I have something to show you!"

Luke went with Miss Davidson to the library. He saw a boy with a big dog!

4

"Luke, this is Hero," said Miss Davidson.
"This is Jamie. Hero is going to come
to school with Jamie every day."

"Why does your dog come to school?"
Luke asked Jamie.
Jamie said, "Hero loves stories.
I think there could be some children at
school who would like to read to him.
Would you like to do that, Luke?"

6

"No! Not me! I can't read very well,"
said Luke.
Jamie said, "Hero loves to look at
pictures, too. Get your reading book,
Luke. It has pictures in it."

7

Luke showed Hero the pictures in
his book. He read some of the story.
Jamie helped him if he couldn't read
a word.

Hero liked Luke's reading.
He got up and Luke saw that
Hero only had three legs!

Jamie told Luke that a long time ago Hero had a very bad accident. He had to learn to walk and run again on three legs.

Luke gave Hero a pat on his ears.
"You didn't give up, did you, Hero?"
he said.

Luke read to Hero every day.
Soon he was reading faster and better.

"I love reading to you, Hero," said Luke.
"I am happy reading now!
I think I'm getting good at it!"

"You are my Reading Hero," Luke said. He gave the dog a big hug. "My friend Megan is not good at reading. Do you want to be her hero, too?"

Hero looked happy. Luke could see that Hero was ready to help Megan.

Soon Megan and Hero were good friend:
Megan was happy about reading, too!